I Was Called Ava

A short story

Abdelkader Ben Rayana

I Was Called Ava

Abdelkader Ben Rayana

No part of this book may be reproduced in any form or by any electronic or mechanical means, including information storage and retrieval systems, without written permission from the author, except for the use of brief quotations in a book review.

This book is a work of fiction. Any resemblance to persons, living or dead, or places, events or locations is purely coincidental. The characters are all productions of the author's imaginations.

Dedication

To those who are struggling with society's stigmas

Foreword

This short story is about courage. Ava Veggie was brave enough to change how people perceived mental health. It wasn't easy having this work written, edited, and published. I struggled with giving the book a title and I have been in doubt whether to publish it or not. In the end, I decided that this work should see the world. I am trying to eliminate, beat, break and why not end the mental health stigma for good with my stories. Ava is the true hope that we would like to see in this world. When I started writing this short story in the summer of 2019, my goal was to shed a light on people who are struggling and let them know that they are not alone.

I hope you will have a great time reading this story because I put my whole soul, heart, and mind into it.

Abdelkader Ben Rayana.

November 2021

Please note: The characters of this short story are British and the events are happening in the United Kingdom, but this story was mostly written in American English.

   'We need to be careful when we talk about people with mental diseases. The mental health stigma is something serious and it should end soon.'

Abdelkader Ben Rayana

I WAS CALLED AVA

'Mom, I want to go to the woods,' I said with my tricky smile.

'You mean the Mersey Forest? It's cold, sweetie. You can go later, and don't be stubborn, especially with me.' Said, my dear mother.

'No, please, Mama, I want to go now.' I insisted.

'Is this real or a dream?' I was asking myself in a gentle whisper.

Maybe it was a dream. It was a good daydream until my psychiatrist diagnosed me with something I didn't understand because I was only thirteen. It was bipolar disorder with psychotic features. I was almost sure of one thing: My mom wanted to take good care of my mental health since I was a toddler. At that age, I had also a wish, a small one but big in the value it could bring. I wanted to work as a school bus driver. This was my only focused goal because I was seeing kids laughing and enjoying their time. I wondered how proud their driver would be to drive them safely to their destination. So, I made up my mind that I would be making more kids happier one day, and I was sure I'd be prouder. My dad was the most encouraging human being I have ever seen. But he made sure that my expectations could be lowered sometimes. He told me that I was his one and only princess. At night, he read me bedtime stories and sang me lullabies. I couldn't sleep for hours, even after those lullabies. I kept thinking that something was wrong with me. I felt like blood was screaming in my veins, my tiny brain was burning, and my bones were aching as though they were breaking. But still, this was a nightmare that I thought I would not wake up from it quickly.

'This is real, and it's forever,' I heard a strange voice saying.

I understood that this voice was trying to confuse me and end my wondering for good. I was terrified to death. I run into the bathroom. I found the bathtub full of water.

'Nobody's home,' The voice kept saying. I got more scared and ran to the safest place, which I consider the colossal library room. I took out two books: The newest DSM and The Diary of a Young Girl by Anne Frank. Unexpectedly, I found our cat, Tutu, crying, and he was pointing at what I could see as a garden full of flowers. From lavenders to big roses and from daisies to cherries still growing. 'But wait for a second, Ava, cherries should not be here.'

***

My classmate Martin was sitting beside me and interrupted me from this nature's beauty. He told me that our French teacher Marguerite was calling out: 'Ava, where did you go with your mind?'

'Nowhere, miss,' I responded, lost.

I realized that I was thinking about what happened last night.

Miss Marguerite was noticing that I was bewildered and asked me to answer a grammar question. Of course, I did not know the answer. The teacher started to get irritated and told me to leave the classroom and not come back until I bring my parent with me to meet her.

Sometimes, things we see and touch can't be so real yet not so fake. An event of this kind had to tell us so.

I couldn't tell my parents. So, I turned to my older brother Nilo who was eighteen. I thought maybe he could do something and be of some help. All he had to say 'Sorry little sista, I can't help you'. And I remembered that he wasn't my parent.

The city of Liverpool seemed quiet after a rainy and thundery night. Nilo wore his beautifully designed old-school jersey with a small Everton logo and an FC Bayern larger logo. This jersey was bought before a soccer game my father attended back in the nineteen-eighties between Everton and Bayern, his favorite team. My dad was and is still an avid fan of the historic club of the German south. Nilo wore the number fifty-two jersey and headed to Goodison park stadium to watch his favorite team face the other blue-colored side, Chelsea. I could see his eyes' enthusiasm, especially the day before home games and when they were played on a Saturday afternoon. I didn't like soccer, but I heard my father and brother discussing games, and they forced me to listen.

I was all on my own as my parents went to one country concert performed by a young American singer who was touring England. Our nanny was having her usual annual holiday. She was South African. From Cape Town, to be exact. Distance mattered to her. She was more than a friend of mine. She called me twice a week through Facetime. I missed her.

The kind of Saturday nights when you get all the comfort you were craving after a long week of stress and routine.

My thoughts were interrupted by seeing the younger version of my mom - maybe because I was looking at her when she was my age - in the living room's photo frame. She looked exactly like me. Perhaps I was looking into the mirror, but I wasn't. I could hear the stadium's crowd through my right ear and the concert in my left ear through the screaming of that girl who was getting weirder every time she got one step closer.

'How on earth could I hear these crowds, and they were about an hour drive from home?'

I stayed awake and fought, with all I could, until Mom came suddenly and I told her about the French class and teacher. She weirdly hugged me and told me softly: 'I'll meet her tomorrow. Don't worry hon. Now go to sleep. It's time for bed'.

I couldn't sleep. Time flew as I was swimming in a pool of thoughts: possibilities and their consequences. The next day seemed heavy but easy.

I saw my mother and my super-elegant professor smiling at each other as though I got the Nobel prize in literature. I didn't say a word until Dad broke the silence on our lunch table after I came me and Mom from school.

'What's up, princess?'

'Ask Mom', I said before a sigh.

'Ava, Nilo go to Riro's restaurant, and I allow you to eat junk food, but only this time', said Mom surprising me, Nilo, and even Dad.

'Don't drink a lot of soft drinks,' She added before we spoke.

'What's the matter?' Nilo managed to say after pushing his plate toward the center of the table, somehow confused but a bit more serious than we used to know him.

'It's just nothing', said Mom.

Nilo was about to leave before Mom told us that the talk would be about me. I left quickly and pretended to go to the restaurant. I went to wash my face to refresh my thoughts. I went to my room passing through our second kitchen.

'We'll take her tomorrow to make sure... to the vet, I mean... maybe'

Mom was talking about me and maybe she was talking about Tutu who was crying. So that's why my parents maybe thought about taking him to the veterinarian. I broke in and told Mom what I heard and she replied 'Yes, we're taking Tutu to the vet. He's crying, laughing, and saying inappropriate things.'

'So that was why you told us to leave the lunch table?', I asked more stunned.

'Because I knew you loved Tutu'.

'Something physical caused him that?'

'No, he has mental health issues. He's depressed'

I just believed the unbelievable quietly. And maybe Tutu wasn't crying or depressed. Maybe he was only growling.

In the end, he was a cat. And I thought that cats didn't get depressed. Maybe he was a dog. Everything seemed possible now.

Tutu was like a little brother to me and Nilo.

That was the last thing I remember before being in my mom's black Range Rover and feeling a bit dizzy. Dad was the one driving. My mom was sitting on my left in the back and took out her Samsung and told me: 'You're a very smart and brave girl. You know that?' Tapping on my shoulder and then she continued: 'I cared about your mental health before you became a teenager'. I just nodded.

'Now I am going to show you something. Some photos and videos of your behavior last night. Do not be surprised sweetheart. I am sure it is a temporary condition. And do not be surprised also because I am going to show this to the doctor. Is that fine with you?'.

I agreed politely.

I was seeing photos and videos of me screaming, shouting, and sometimes talking to myself. I was verbally aggressive once or twice. I was cursing. I never imagined myself once in my life that I would curse, even though they were only one or two words. I looked as if I was drunk. I was really ashamed in front of Mom who was looking comfortable. The video played for about two minutes and I was starting to get upset, but rather uncomfortable. The greeneries at the window made me feel a bit better. The video played for ten more seconds and then I saw 'MYSELF' choking Tutu and Nilo was stopping me while saying: 'What is wrong with you Ava now?'

My dad wasn't in the video but I could hear him talking in a low voice to Mom.

'ENOUGH' I screamed, letting go of my mom's hand. She said nothing and then stopped the video and showed me a photo that shocked me.

'I took this photo after the video' Said Mom

I saw myself wearing my pink swimming clothes in front of the house in that freezing weather.

'You were dancing darling wearing those clothes in a three Celsius temperature'

'Oh My God, Mom why are you torturing me? I don't want to see anything more of this sort'

I brushed my golden hair, closed my olive-green eyes, leaned my head against the window, and prayed in silence.

'Your daughter is experiencing some kind of mental disorder. Acute episodes of mood swings and psychosis. Auditory and visual hallucinations while having a manic episode.'

'Ava, my colleague doctor Sam diagnosed you with bipolar disorder with psychotic features and he was probably right' He continued after turning his gaze to me.

'What I can assure of, Madam is that Ava will be better in a matter of a few years. I want to treat the symptoms rather than talk only about the diagnosis'

I covered my face with my small hands and let out a choked sigh and a violent sob.

*****

I was on more meds a few hours after I met the psychiatrist. They reduced somehow the mood swings and the psychosis. And guess what: 'I started blogging'.

I blogged for days and days. I wrote about mental health in general and in-depth and about my symptoms and struggles, and I met many young people like me from all over Britain and Europe. I video chatted with them.

The medicines helped. I returned to reality through the narrow tunnel of persistence and patience.

I was driving the bus I dreamed of driving. Not the yellow bus though. It was the green one. I chose it on purpose. This color represented mental health. Just like the pink color for breast cancer.

I loved to wear the green ribbon too, it was the international symbol for mental health awareness.

I was attending community meetings in private and public hospitals and clinics. I was able to see the theory put into practice.

Giving up was not an option and I started to feel better.

I got my high school certificate with an average grade. I was a full-time school bus driver soon after that. I won on all sides. Sometimes I struggled with self-control that only mental health survivors could understand.

I wrote this text for me and whoever struggling with a mental health problem. It's a small message which includes one life experience and memory and it's posted on my blog:

Fight with the resources you have I will try to end or at least break the mental health stigma.

My maternal aunt and my friend since kindergarten days stopped talking to me when they both heard that I was sick. That was the pure definition of stigma. They were ashamed. I did expect that.

Ava Veggie wasn't my real name. My real name was Alexa Twain. I liked Ava more. Ava was a name derived from a childhood 'trauma' that motivated me to be the girl I am now.

My dad suffered from Osteoarthritis but he kept working as a gardener in his friend's house.

I was trying to free myself from the bizarre looks of other people who did not understand what mental illness was. I thought that they didn't even understand what it felt like to have it, despite I was normal, doing quite well.

Ending or at least eliminating this stigma even a great part of it, wasn't easy. I had another solution. Music was the one. I hired three

non-famous folk bands from all over England to perform in small concerts in high schools, universities, and mental hospitals. Thank God, I was supported by my parents' money. Other school bus drivers supported me too.

They were two girls and one young man. They had been singing songs about mental health since the beginning of the twenty-first century.

I realized after the concerts that I should buy books -fiction and non-fiction- talking about mental health and ending its stigma, read them, and then donate them.

One day you would say I did it because I struggled enough to reach the very end. So, you should reach it too. Maybe I am stupid, dumb or whatever but I will fight with all I had until I succeed. I could see my friends looking at me on the bus with their wide eyes as though I was trying to hurt them with the small 'innocent' van. It was the bus. An old one but it spoke to me through its steering wheel. I took a break whenever I could.

Now let me tell you a story about the childhood trauma that caused me to be called by everyone "Ava".

One time when I was two years and four days old. I was following my dad's steps towards his friend's garden. It was full of cherries. He was driving a tractor as a hobby to help his friend plant the new seeds. I was left behind, sobbing. Maybe it was a dream. Sometimes reality hurts more than a living nightmare. Dad drove the tractor some steps forward. Unexpectedly, I fell. I was under the tractor; my dad didn't notice me and the tractor was all over me. It was a small tractor though. A cute one. Dad heard me screaming. He stopped and took me to the doctor. This doctor was a general practitioner, and he happened to be the friend who had the cherries garden.

'It's just *A Vegetable Accident*', he told my dad

You saw how I wrote it. Three initials: A, V, and A. The name Ava came from there. My Dad asked him: 'A vegetables accident?'.

'Are you making fun of me or what?' My dad continued shouting.

'No, I am not making fun of you, but take it from me: Your daughter will be called Ava Veggie since it was a vegetable accident.'

His sarcasm was killing my father.

We never heard any news from this friend after this "horrible" incident.

It wasn't that horrible, I didn't have big scars. Or even small ones. Some blood was on my face. That was it. But the way this friend behaved was so insulting. He didn't even examine me.

'A hobby could turn against you', my dad told me a bit after we left.

'I decided to call you Ava Veggie, it's easier than Alexa Twain which will become your second name, and also remember that those unpleasant memories can help you become stronger, my dear beloved Ava.' He continued.

Anyways, I didn't remember his name or where he came from, and I didn't talk to my father or even my mother about this incident ever since.

***

Breaking the mental health stigma was a task that I had to do with a bunch of bloggers from Liverpool. When I started blogging, I didn't have the intention to have a great following. The last time I checked, only last week, I had 105,484 followers, and that made me motivated to start my own website.

As I was writing my last post on my blog and organizing my website. I received a message from someone called "The Green Professor 65". Maybe he or she was born in that year.

The message said: 'Hello, we have met years ago. Let me see you soon. We need to talk. You know where to find me.'

I was a bit shocked because it was the first time that I received such a message. When I went to check the person's profile, I found out that he was male, but there wasn't any photo of him.

I didn't bother much and closed my tiny laptop.

***

I was seeing a woman in a grey dress. She was young and beautiful. It was in a garden full of red roses. The woman spoke in a thick British accent telling me that I was welcomed at her house as much as I wanted. We were only me and her in there.

Suddenly and out of the blue, this woman started to scream and she told me that she wanted to adopt me.

'I don't have a daughter. I can't have children. I am sick, I have cancer. Uterine cancer, to be exact'

'What do I have to do? I have my parents and brother. I want to live with them. I am sorry, I can't be your daughter. I can't live with you.'

'Well, your parents and your brother died in an accident yesterday while driving to their favorite restaurant.'

'Oh no, that can't be possible. You don't know anything about that.'

'Well, look at this newspaper: A MOTHER, A FATHER, AND THEIR SON WERE KILLED IN A CAR ACCIDENT WHILE DRIVING IN LIVERPOOL. And it's published in one of the Manchester-based papers.'

I was in shock as I read the article and saw their photos. She was right.

'Now that you are left alone without anyone, you should come to live with me as my daughter'

'Who said you didn't kill them?'

'Me, oh no. I am a good woman and since I was diagnosed with cancer I haven't gotten out of my house. Now can you be my daughter?'

'I told you no. NO, NO, AND NO. PERIOD.'

'You are my dear daughter now anyways, aren't you?'

'Will you let go of me?' I told the woman who pressed my hand so hard.

My hand was aching. I wanted to let go of her so badly but I couldn't. I had only one solution, and it was to push her so that my hand would be set free and she could get out of my way.

I tried pushing her, and she fell on the floor, her head hit the bottom part of the bunching table in the living room, and blood was coming out of her head like a flowing river. The last words she screamed were: 'AVA, AVA, AVA'

'What have I done?' I shouted

I wanted to check her pulse and I was shocked when I knew that she passed away. I didn't mean to end her life.

As I was leaving, I was surprised by a man. A familiar face but I didn't know who exactly.

I couldn't leave, I was stuck under a tractor in the garden. The red roses were all gathered like dead, pale people in there.

The sound of the woman was still in my ears 'AVA, AVA, AVA...'

'AVA, AVA, AVA wake up, wake up.'

It was my dear mother.

'What happened to you daughter? You were dreaming or what? I heard you screaming from the living room'

I kept silent then I managed to say in a low and weak voice: 'I don't know.'

Indeed, I wasn't sure if it was a dream or if I was hallucinating. I hoped that I didn't relapse again. I was lying down on my bed, the laptop on my stomach. I assumed it was a dream but it was real and vivid. That had to mean something. Something which I didn't have a single clue about.

I was anxious because I thought that I might have done something wrong. Did I kill her?

I was in complete doubt.

***

The next day, I wanted to check ''The Green Professor 65'' again but suddenly I was surprised by him deleting his blog account. So, it was the only way where he could reach me since he didn't know my email and I didn't have social media.

I just searched for 'The Green Professor 1965' on Google and the first thing that popped up was The University of Liverpool. I clicked on the link and I saw About the Professor: Abdelghani Wood.

He was a doctor in Clinical Psychology. I couldn't help my curiosity and clicked on more info. It showed his five books in clinical psychology, cognitive-behavioral therapy (CBT), and hypnosis.

And I remembered that Nilo just applied to many universities to do his masters and one of them was the University of Liverpool.

I felt something strange but good was going to happen and I had a feeling that this man was someone who knew me from school or my childhood.

It was a Sunday; all universities were on the weekend break.

On Monday morning, I took my mother's car and went to the university but before that, I checked the professor's office hours on the website. He had office hours on Mondays and Tuesdays from noon till three.

It was ten o'clock on the dot. So, I had to wait for two more hours.

I waited in the sun. It was a good sunny day. Students were on bikes traveling around the campus chatting, laughing, and shouting.

I went to the cafeteria to have a latte. It was the first time in a long while that I had a coffee.

I tried not to look nervous, and finally, it was noon.

I was in front of the office. The door was closed, and it had a paper on it: 'WENT FOR LUNCH... BACK AT 12:20'

They were the slowest twenty minutes of my whole life, and finally, all I could hear was the footsteps of someone. It was a female university student, and I knew immediately that she came to see the professor.

We exchanged Hellos and she asked me if I was waiting for Professor Wood. I told her that I wanted to see him, and then I asked her where he came from she told me that he was Pakistani–British.

And finally, a shadow appeared a few seconds after and it had to be him.

I saw a man who was not very tall and not very short, skinny, he got a tan recently, which made his white face skin look more attractive with freckles. His eyes and hair were brown, and he was wearing a white polo with small green dots, beige trousers, and shoes.

He managed to say to me: 'Hey, you must be Ava, we will have a lengthy talk later but let me see my student first. You can sit in the other chair or on that sofa and listen to my student's questions'

The student advanced and was wearing a shy smile. She asked the professor some questions about the last class session. They were questions about clinical psychology principles. She was hungry for knowledge.

She started to leave and before reaching the door, she turned around and said: 'Will there be four or five chapters in the quiz, professor?'

'Only four. The fifth will be included in the exam along with chapters six and seven. Seven of them will be included in the exam inshallah'

'Sounds clear. Thank you.'

'Sure'

The girl left, the professor closed his notebook and turned back from his computer to me.

'She is an excellent student of mine and I have to agree that all my students are smart like her. I am teaching a Ph.D. course and a principles course in clinical psychology as you may have noticed, and I go to one of the psychiatric hospitals in Liverpool on Wednesdays and Thursdays to see my patients. I work as a clinical psychologist in there.'

'I see' I replied quite dazzled with his confidence.

'How are you doing Ava?' He continued, asking with enthusiasm.

'Well, well.'

'You haven't changed much, Ava' Said Dr. Wood after widening his eyes.

'Where have we met? I have met many people but I think I might have met you in school.' I said, more curious.

'Not exactly, can you guess now?'

'I am not good at guessing. Can you please tell me?'

'Okay, your dad had been a good friend of mine for a long time before he got offended about what I said to...'

'I think I know now, you are the general practitioner who had the cherries garden and called my incident: A vegetables accident' I interrupted.

'Wow, you remember well and that is ace. I will tell you my whole story and how I got to find you again. I need to talk to your father soon.'

'Go ahead, tell me.' I managed to say feeling quite uncomfortable.

'Okay, your dad and even your mom know very well that I was a true friend and that I studied medicine and clinical psychology in Scotland. I started as a general practitioner then I became a clinical psychologist. I was born in Karachi, Pakistan in 1965 and moved from there with my parents when I was four months of age. I studied in Scotland until my first year of uni, and then transferred to the University of Birmingham. My grades were beyond great. It was in the mid-eighties when I met your father during a visit to Liverpool. He was a modest man and had too much pride in everything he does, which made him humbler and a man of great value. A simple man in a good way, I can say. I am hoping that he is still the same man I knew. I was the one who introduced him to your mother. She had a crush on him but she was too shy to tell him, so I had to be the one who helped her get to him.'

I was smiling almost giggling when I heard this story for the first time.

Doctor Wood smiled slowly and then continued: 'They got married and had Nilo soon after that. I think Nilo remembers my name. A few years after, you were born, and I was still the best friend to the family until that incident. That event had a special story behind it.'

The Pakistani–British man sighed and then managed to say: 'I had a wife from Manchester and she was the only woman that I loved. A true and rare love. Unfortunately, she was infertile, and her main dream was to heal that and have a daughter. She wanted to name her daughter, Ava. She loved that name. It was the first name of her favorite novelist. Books, the cherries we had in the garden, and gardening were her escape from a painful reality. She was an airline stewardess, and when we got married she left her job and decided to take care of herself and our house,'

'One afternoon, she returned home sobbing and called me when I was at work. I knew that something was wrong from the tone of her voice. She told me that she had to see me. I hurried to the house and she told me that her doctor informed her that she had womb cancer. I couldn't believe it. I hugged her and I cried in front of her which I shouldn't have done.' Dr. Wood sighed and felt uneasy then he was pointing at her photo which was on one of the bookshelves.

When I saw her photo, I felt something right under my skin, as if my blood was freezing.

It was the exact woman whom I saw the day before while I was hallucinating or dreaming.

I screamed quickly: 'I think I have something to tell you.'

'What is that?'

'I need to tell you that I know your wife and an accident happened when I visited her.'

'What accident?' Mr. Abdelghani asked, startled.

'I saw your wife. I don't know but I think I killed her. It was yesterday.'

'I hope you are joking because my wife died almost two decades ago of cancer'

'Oh really? Because I think my bizarre daydreams and psychosis returned. That's a relief though'

'I see. But, you don't have to believe them'

'You know that they are vivid and I see things that are close to reality.'

'And have you done anything about them?'

'Not really, I am on meds. They help but not completely. I have to cope anyway. You can finish your story.'

'Ok, so after the death of Emma, your dad had to console me and take care of the garden and the cherries -as a hobby- a few months after the passing of my wife and only lover. One day and it was the first and only day he brought you and that accident or incident happened. I didn't find the right words so I said what I said.'

'The name Ava was in my mind even though your name was Alexa. Your dad knew about Emma's dream which was that she loved that name. He decided to give you that name because he liked it too. I forgot about that incident until last week when I was reading an article online on mental health stigma. I saw that some bloggers are changing Liverpool, the UK, and even Europe. I saw Ava Veggie and your photo, and I recognized you immediately. I had to reach you and send you a message. I couldn't reveal my name, or photo otherwise you wouldn't come to meet me if you knew me. So, I had to approach you differently, and here we are.'

I was surprised and I had to admit that this man was a decent man. I stayed silent for a few seconds then and I told him: 'I am speechless. This story inspired me to write it on my blog. I will change the names so that it will protect privacy. I will call the blog post **"I WAS CALLED AVA"**'

The professor agreed and told me: 'No need to change the names, I want people to know my story and my name through you and know why you were called Ava.'

I returned home and I wrote the post of almost a thousand words. It was trending in Liverpool and the whole UK for a complete week. It had almost thirteen million views. Even my parents read it, and while I was in my room, I heard some knocking on my door. It was my father. He stepped in and told me with a triumphant tone: 'I am proud of you princess. First of all, I am proud of your blog and how you are raising awareness on mental health and also because you changed my opinion about Dr. Wood. I need to see him and apologize.'

My father started talking again to his friend and I was delighted about that.

A few weeks after, I started going to therapy again, and Dr. Wood became my psychologist.

I had to agree that I improved tremendously with the sessions. The weird daydreams, mood swings, psychosis, and hallucinations disappeared almost completely.

***

My blog and website got more popular in the UK, Europe, and over 134 countries in total. I received lots of feedback, messages, and letters which mentioned mostly that they are proud of me and that now they are perceiving mental health differently.

The stigma was less among my acquaintances, but it didn't subside.

Most importantly, to live with mental diseases was like living with a family member or a pet.

But, the sickness should be forgotten as it's not advised to always talk about the diagnoses or symptoms.

I realized that mental health stigma could be ended in a matter of a few decades or centuries. Who knows?

The End

Afterword

I hope you enjoyed reading this short story and that you related well to the events and characters.

Find all my books on Amazon and try to leave an honest review on Amazon and Goodreads.

Thank you.

Abdelkader Ben Rayana.

November 2021

Acknowledgment

I would like to express my gratitude to my parents Sonia and Chekib for their continuous support.

Many thanks to my brother Fares who reviewed the last drafts of this work.

I also appreciate the help of the fellow author and friend Ellen Khodakivska for reading one of the last drafts of this story.

I want also to thank my readers for believing in me and for being one of the sources of my inspiration.

About the author

Abdelkader Ben Rayana is a young Tunisian author. He was born in 1994 in Tunis and now he is living in UAE. In 2018, he started writing his debut novel Shining Dreams: The Roots and self-published it in 2020. He devotes his time to writing and editing his future works, including Novels, Short Stories, Poems & Lyrics collections, Novelettes, Novellas, and Children's books. He is also reading some books.

Find Abdelkader Ben Rayana on Twitter and Instagram: @abdelkaderbr